SKY HIGH

Written by Anne Myers

Illustrated by Wendy Shaul

STECK-VAUGHN
ELEMENTARY · SECONDARY · ADULT · LIBRARY

A Harcourt Classroom Education Company

www.steck-vaughn.com

"Hello, my friends!" said Kip the bird.
"I have good news. Have you heard?

Beyond those mountains lies Sky-Top,
A place where frogs can swim and hop.

Where chipmunks feast on nuts and cherries,
And birds can fill their nests with berries."

"It sounds like just the place for us."
Fritz the frog said, "Let's take a bus."

"There are no roads that go that high."
Kip said, "You two will have to fly.

Let's fly to Sky-Top by balloon.
We'll get there by this afternoon."

They packed a basket with supplies,
Food for Fritz, like worms and flies.

Amos Chipmunk brought a treat,
Lots of acorns that he could eat.

"I'll just bring some seeds," said Kip.
"And now we're ready for our trip."

They cut the ropes and waved good-bye.
Then up they went, into the sky!

Over yards and homes they flew.
How small the world looked from that view.

They couldn't hear a single noise.
The trains and buses looked like toys.

Kip shouted, "Mountain tops! See?
That is where we want to be."

Just then the wind began to blow.
The basket soon filled up with snow!

They wrapped themselves in lots of clothes
And jumped about and rubbed their toes.

6

They tried to land, but soon a breeze
Carried them off into some trees.

Kip said, "We are not high enough."
And so they started tossing stuff.

They threw out boxes, trinkets, keys,
Until their basket cleared the trees.

Kip called out, "Where can we be?"
Fritz said, "We're headed out to sea."

And sure enough, they heard the sound
Of crashing waves from all around.

They waved hello to all the whales
Who smiled at them and flipped their tails.

Fritz said, "Can you hear that noisy fuss?
What could seagulls want from us?"

Finally Amos used some words
That seemed to scare the greedy birds.

"Stop that pecking! Shoo, birds, shoo!
There isn't any food for you!"

 9

The seagulls stopped their noisy riot,
And once again the air was quiet.

"Whew!" said Fritz. "It might be best
If all of us could take a rest."

The crew had just dropped off to sleep
When their radio began to beep.

"Get ready for a rocky ride!" yelled Kip.
"Take cover! Everybody hide!"

They held on tight and watched the sky.
Then, ZOOM! An airplane roared on by.

The basket shook, the crew spun around,
But all three friends were safe and sound.

 11

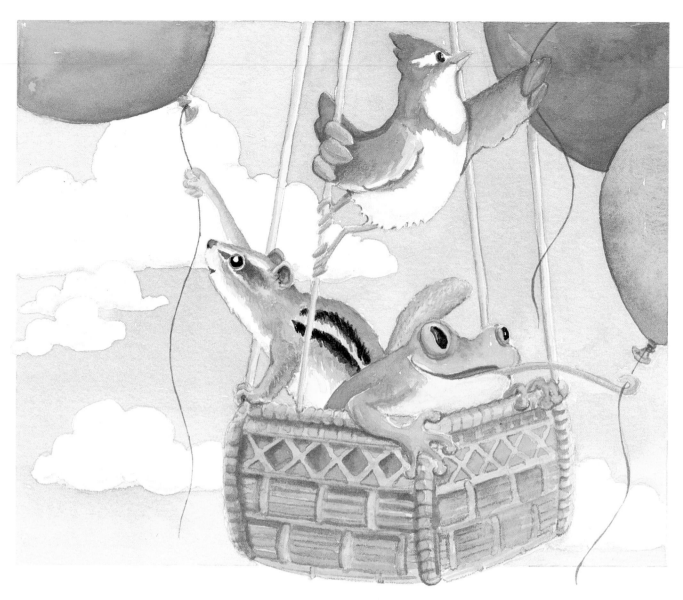

"The sky's not clear yet," said the crew.
"What's this green and pink and blue?"

Amos said, "They're round as moons.
I think they're children's lost balloons!"

Then Kip said, "Let's catch all three,
A balloon for Amos, Fritz, and me."

Fritz heard a sound. "Uh-oh. What's that?
Did I hear a drop or splat?"

Then something wet flew past his ear.
"What could be flying way up here?

It's not a bird. It's not a plane.
It looks and feels just like rain!"

13

A cold north wind began to wail.
And then the raindrops turned to hail.

BOING! The crew put helmets on
Until the wind and hail were gone.

They fended off the storm at last,
But their balloon was sinking fast.

14

Fritz yelled, "Grab a balloon, now we must go!"
Then they jumped into the sky below.

The three enjoyed a quiet ride
Above the lovely countryside.

Where they'd land, they did not know,
As they drifted through the snow.

Thump! They landed on the ground.
They stretched their legs and looked around.

A sign said **WELCOME TO SKY-TOP.**
At last, this was their final stop.

Kip said, "We're here. Isn't it grand?
What a great place this is to land."